P9-BAU-195

TRUE LIES

18 TALES
FOR YOU TO JUDGE

TOLD BY
GEORGE SHANNON

ILLUSTRATED BY
JOHN O'BRIEN

BEECH TREE
NEW YORK

Copyright © 1997 by George W. B. Shannon
Illustrations copyright © 1997 by John O'Brien

All rights reserved. No part of this book may be reproduced or
utilized in any form or by any means, electronic or mechanical,
including photocopying, recording, or by any information
storage and retrieval system, without permission in
writing from the Publisher.

Published by Greenwillow Books
a division of William Morrow & Company, Inc.
1350 Avenue of the Americas, New York, N Y 10019
www.williammorrow.com

Printed in the United States of America.

The Library of Congress has cataloged the Greenwillow Books
edition of *True Lies* as follows:
Shannon, George.
True lies / told by George Shannon; pictures by John O'Brien.
p. cm.
Summary: Presents a collection of eighteen brief folktales in
which the reader is asked to explain how the folk characters
lied and told the truth at the same time.
ISBN 0-688-14483-7
1. Tales.   [1. Folklore.   2. Literary recreations.]   I. O'Brien,
John, ill.   II. Title.   PZ8.1.S495Tr 1997   398.2—dc20   [E]
96-7149   CIP AC

First Beech Tree Edition, 1998
ISBN 0-688-16371-8
10 9 8 7 6 5 4 3 2 1

FOR DAVID HOLTER

—G. S.

FOR TESS

—J. O'B.

CONTENTS

INTRODUCTION

*W*e are all taught to tell the truth. But anyone who has watched the action in a courtroom, been misled by a commercial, read a newspaper headline, or been tricked by a sly classmate knows that sometimes truths are lies in disguise. Telling the truth can be very different than telling the *whole* truth and nothing but the truth. People may state a truth, but by leaving out certain details they may not be telling the *whole* truth, which means what they've said is also a lie. Other sly talkers use words and phrases that can have double meanings. They tell the truth, but *we* create the lie when we jump to the wrong conclusion. Some people are even trickier and tell the truth in a way that *sounds* like a lie.

These folktales and jokes from around the world all play with slippery truths and lies in disguise. By reading carefully and not jumping to conclusions, you will discover how these folk characters lie while at the same time they tell the truth.

1.
One Cookie

Nate and Anna wanted to bake cookies and asked their mother over and over and over again till she finally agreed.

"You may bake them," she said. "But you may eat only one cookie each before dinner. Just one. And no eating cookie dough, either. Or anything else. I don't want you spoiling your appetite."

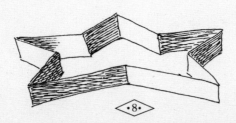

Nate and Anna agreed, but at dinner both were too full to eat.

"You promised to eat only one cookie each," scolded their mother.

"And that's all we had," both insisted. "Just one."

"And no cookie dough?"

The brother and sister shook their heads no.

"Honest," said Nate. "We ate only one cookie each and nothing else."

What's the truth, the whole truth?
And where's the lie?

THE WHOLE TRUTH

Nate and Anna were telling the truth.
Except, that is, for the size
of their one cookie each.
Each had made a single cookie
large enough to cover
an entire cookie sheet.

2. The Donkey and the Carrots

Several fellows were swapping riddles as they sat around the potbellied stove.

"Once," said Jim, "there was a donkey tied to a rope that was eight feet long, and there was also a wagon of carrots thirty yards away. That donkey loved carrots more than words can say, and he got them, too! Any guesses how he did it?"

"Gnawed through the rope?" said a man.

"Nope."

"It's impossible," said another.

"Nope."

"You're lying," said a third.

But Jim's best friend shook his head and smiled. "He's telling the truth. I saw it myself. Even though the donkey was tied to a rope only eight feet long, he got those carrots in the wagon thirty yards away."

What's the truth, the whole truth?
And where's the lie?

THE WHOLE TRUTH

Jim never said
that the other end of
the eight-foot-long rope
was tied to anything.
The donkey just walked
to the carrots.

3.
Ropedancing

One summer Tyll Eulenspiegel decided to earn some money by dancing on a rope as he'd seen others do in the traveling shows. After a few days' practice he was so good others were jealous of the coins he earned. Two boys even cut into his rope so it broke the next time he tried to perform.

"Ha! Look at the great ropedancer now!" The boys laughed.

Tyll calmly retied the rope and made them a wager.

"Give me your shoes—whatever their size—and I'll dance with them up here on the rope. If I fail, you'll get all the money I've earned today. If I succeed, everyone here owes me a coin."

The boys knew Tyll couldn't dance on a rope wearing shoes that didn't fit. He'd trip and fall in seconds. They eagerly tossed him their shoes. Soon others tossed up their shoes as well.

Tyll danced along the rope as he caught their shoes,
then bowed and announced, "Please put your money
in the hat below."

"Not until you do what you bargained to do!" called
the boys.

"Ah, but I have." Tyll laughed. "Pay up."

Though the boys continued to argue, everyone else
in the crowd knew Tyll was right.

What's the truth, the whole truth?
And where's the lie?

THE WHOLE TRUTH

Tyll wagered he would dance
with their shoes on the rope,
which he did by dancing
and juggling with them.
He never wagered that he would
dance *in* their shoes or wear them.

4. Half
the Cherries

In times past farmers were often so busy harvesting hay, they didn't have time to pick their cherries, which ripened at the same time. To make sure the cherries didn't go to waste, farmers hired someone else to pick them, giving half the cherries as pay.

One year a busy farmer's trees
were so laden with cherries, he was
glad when a neighbor said, "If I may
have half the cherries, I'll pick them today."
"It's a deal!"
The neighbor quickly set to work and was
gone by the time the farmer came in from the
fields. When he couldn't find his half of the cherries,
the farmer went to the neighbor's house.

"Where's my half?" he demanded.

"On the tree."

"The tree? You said you'd pick them all for the half. You lied!"

"Did not," said the neighbor. "I did exactly as I said."

What's the truth, the whole truth?
And where's the lie?

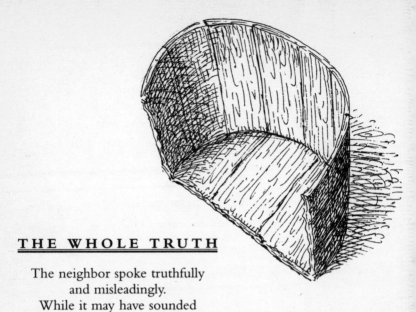

THE WHOLE TRUTH

The neighbor spoke truthfully
and misleadingly.
While it may have sounded
as if he said he'd pick the cherries
for half in pay, he actually said
if he could have half,
then he would pick *them*,
meaning *his* half.

5. A Little Land

In ancient times the brothers Joseph and David searched for a place to settle and build a new village for their friends and families. But as soon as officials discovered they were Jews, the brothers would be turned away.

At last one governor agreed to give the brothers a small piece of land, but a piece so small he thought they'd be insulted and refuse the offer.

"You may have a plot of land," proclaimed the governor. "But it can be no larger than what can be surrounded by the hide of a large ox."

To the governor's surprise, the brothers agreed. The next day they marked off enough land to build a few homes and a synagogue.

"This is impossible," announced the governor. "An outrage! You've broken your word."

The brothers assured him they'd only marked off land as he told them to do.

"We've only taken what you promised to give."

What's the truth, the whole truth?
And where's the lie?

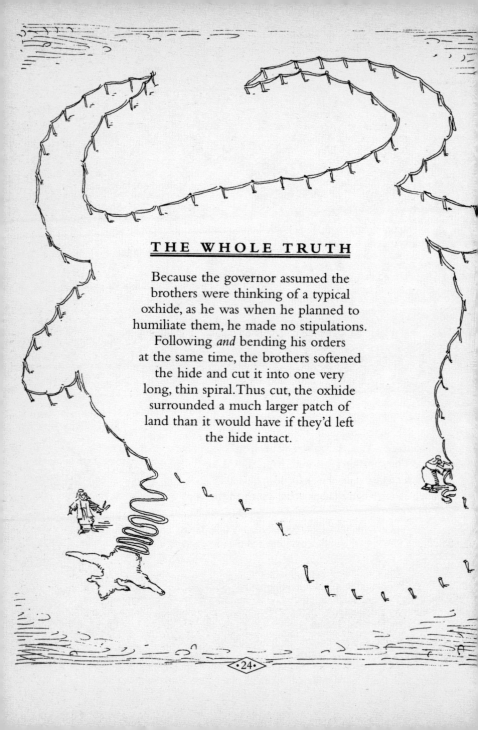

THE WHOLE TRUTH

Because the governor assumed the
brothers were thinking of a typical
oxhide, as he was when he planned to
humiliate them, he made no stipulations.
Following *and* bending his orders
at the same time, the brothers softened
the hide and cut it into one very
long, thin spiral. Thus cut, the oxhide
surrounded a much larger patch of
land than it would have if they'd left
the hide intact.

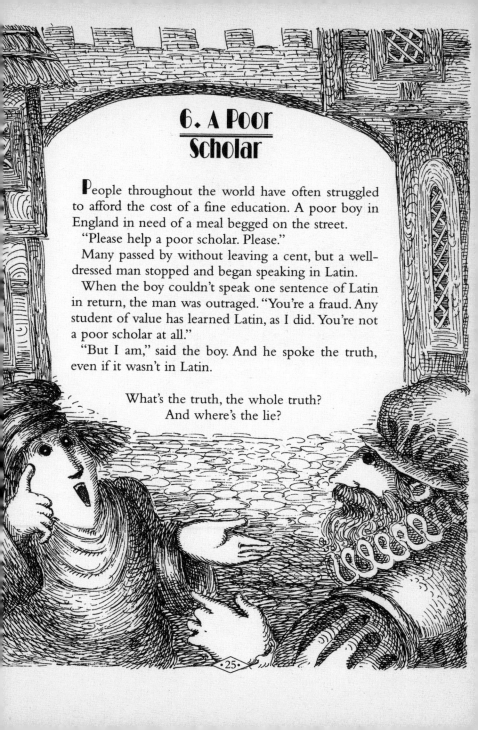

6. A Poor Scholar

People throughout the world have often struggled to afford the cost of a fine education. A poor boy in England in need of a meal begged on the street.

"Please help a poor scholar. Please."

Many passed by without leaving a cent, but a well-dressed man stopped and began speaking in Latin.

When the boy couldn't speak one sentence of Latin in return, the man was outraged. "You're a fraud. Any student of value has learned Latin, as I did. You're not a poor scholar at all."

"But I am," said the boy. And he spoke the truth, even if it wasn't in Latin.

What's the truth, the whole truth?
And where's the lie?

THE WHOLE TRUTH

The well-dressed man was assuming
the boy meant a *financially* poor student.
The boy, while poor, also meant
"poor scholar" as a way of saying
"bad student"—and proved it
by not knowing Latin.

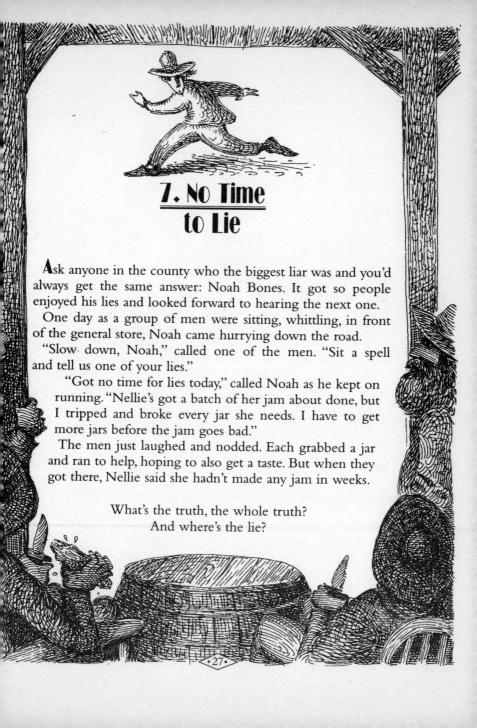

7. No Time to Lie

Ask anyone in the county who the biggest liar was and you'd always get the same answer: Noah Bones. It got so people enjoyed his lies and looked forward to hearing the next one.

One day as a group of men were sitting, whittling, in front of the general store, Noah came hurrying down the road.

"Slow down, Noah," called one of the men. "Sit a spell and tell us one of your lies."

"Got no time for lies today," called Noah as he kept on running. "Nellie's got a batch of her jam about done, but I tripped and broke every jar she needs. I have to get more jars before the jam goes bad."

The men just laughed and nodded. Each grabbed a jar and ran to help, hoping to also get a taste. But when they got there, Nellie said she hadn't made any jam in weeks.

What's the truth, the whole truth?
And where's the lie?

THE WHOLE TRUTH

When Noah told the men
he didn't have time to tell a lie,
he was telling a lie.
Nellie wasn't making any jam.

8. Lost
Money

A poor young man searched the streets each day for anything he could find to trade for food. One day he found not only a big horn from a bull but also a bag of money. He ran to the priest and asked what he should do.

"Carry the money through the streets," advised the priest, "and keep asking if anyone has lost it. If no one claims it, then it is yours to keep."

That evening the young man returned to the priest with the bag of money.

"Did you carry it through the streets as I told you to do?"

"Yes," said the young man. "I called and called, 'Has anyone lost this?' but no one claimed it."

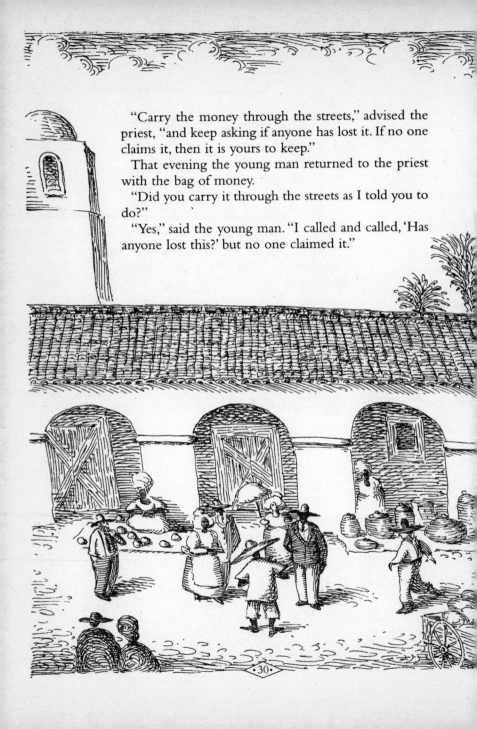

"No one?" asked the priest, shaking his head.

"No one," said the young man, "which means the money is all mine to keep."

The priest believed the young man was telling the truth, but still couldn't believe no one had claimed the bag of coins as theirs.

What's the truth, the whole truth?
And where's the lie?

THE WHOLE TRUTH

The young man carried the bag of money
around town, but he did so with the bag inside
the bull's horn where no one could see it.
When he called out, "Has anyone lost this?"
they assumed he meant the horn.
He'd been careful *not* to ask,
"Has anyone lost this money?"

9.
All Mine

After their wedding a bride and groom took a wagon ride to see the groom's house and farm they'd now share.

"See those cows over yonder?" the groom said as he stroked his whiskers proudly. "Well, all these are mine."

"See those sheep over yonder?" he said a bit later, stroking his whiskers again. "All these are mine."

Another mile down the road they drove up to a ratty old shack.

"Home sweet home," said the farmer.

"What!" cried the bride. "You expect me to live here when you've got all those cows and sheep? You can afford a better house than this."

"No, I can't. This is all I own."

"Then why have you been lying?"

"Never have. Not once."

What's the truth, the whole truth?
And where's the lie?

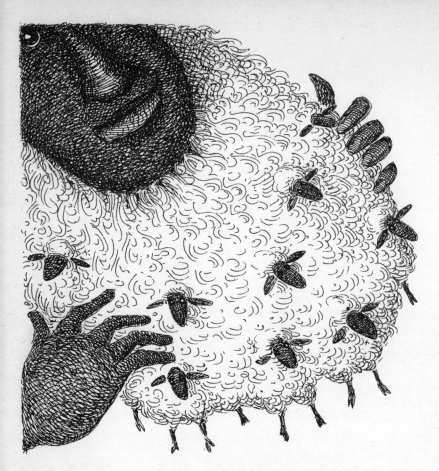

THE WHOLE TRUTH

Each time the farmer said,
"All these are mine," he meant
the whiskers he was stroking.
He never said the animals were his—
though many would say he helped
the bride jump to that conclusion.

10. Matti and Peikko

In the olden days of Finland Peikko the gnome loved spending time with humans, especially Matti. Peikko and Matti were always trying to out-do and out-trick each other. They were equals at playing tricks, but at dances women left Peikko alone and rushed to dance with handsome Matti.

Peikko was determined that one day he'd get to dance every dance. When he heard a wedding dance was being planned, Peikko ran to ask Matti a favor.

"Please, Matti, will you guard the door of my cellar this Saturday night? I have to be gone and can't risk anyone stealing my sacks of gold. I trust you more than anyone else."

"Of course," promised Matti. "For you I'd do anything."

Peikko nearly danced right then with the news. Matti could be full of trouble, but he'd never broken his word.

That Saturday Peikko danced every dance at the wedding and was having the time of his life till he turned and saw all the women running toward Matti.

"Liar!" yelled Peikko. "You're not supposed to be here. You promised to guard my cellar tonight."

"Why would I do that when I knew there might be a dance tonight?"

"But you promised."

"No, I didn't."

In minutes everyone there was taking a side in the argument.

What's the truth, the whole truth?
And where's the lie?

THE WHOLE TRUTH

Matti had never promised
to guard Peikko's cellar.
Peikko had asked him to guard the door
of his cellar, and Matti was doing that.
He had brought the door to the dance
so he could guard it.

11.
A Tall Hog

A farmer once took a truckload of blue-ribbon hogs to the fair. But all he talked about was the hog he'd left at home.

"*That* hog is so tall," he explained as he held his hand high, "that a fellow can't touch its back if he holds his hand as high as he can."

With all that talk a man soon offered to buy the other hog. The price was settled, the man paid, and the two men started back to the farm to fetch the hog.

"There it is!" said the farmer.

"*That* hog?" said the man as he stared at a regular hog. "You lied!"

"Did not."

"But you said—"

"The truth," interrupted the farmer. "Just think for a minute and you'll know I did."

What's the truth, the whole truth?
And where's the lie?

THE WHOLE TRUTH

The farmer spoke the truth
while at the same time
he led the buyer to believe a lie.
A fellow *can't* touch the hog's back
if he holds his hand as high as he can—
because the hog is a regular-sized hog.

12. Love and Pumpkins

When the king announced he was going to marry, stories of the bride quickly spread through the palace.

"She's beautiful," said one servant.

"With the voice of a bird," said another.

"More than that," said a third. "She can do anything! When the king dared her to get a large pumpkin inside a narrow-necked jar without cutting the pumpkin or breaking the jar, she did it. My cousin was there when the king broke open the jar."

"That's impossible. Your cousin is nothing but lies," said a servant just joining the group.

"No, it's true," said another. "I heard the king announce it myself."

What's the truth, the whole truth?
And where's the lie?

THE WHOLE TRUTH

It is true the bride got a large pumpkin
inside a narrow-necked jar
without cutting the pumpkin
or breaking the jar.
Since the king did not say she had
to *start* with a large pumpkin,
the bride placed a tiny pumpkin
inside the jar, then let it grow
while it was still attached to the vine.

13. Shoes and Peas

Two Talmudic students went to the rabbi and confessed that they had sinned.

"We must make amends. What can we do to atone?"

After hearing the details of the students' sins, the rabbi rattled a bag of chickpeas and told the students to put a handful of peas in each of their shoes.

"Perhaps after walking for ten days on these peas, you'll think before you sin again."

The two students went to their respective homes and followed the rabbi's orders. A few days later when they met again, the first student was hobbling in pain from the dried peas in his shoes. The other student, however, walked with ease and a smile on his face.

"How dare you disobey the rabbi's order to put peas in your shoes!" said the first student.

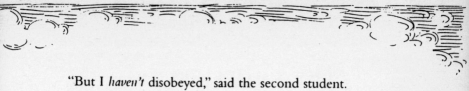

"But I *haven't* disobeyed," said the second student.

"Impossible," said the first. "I can barely walk because of these peas in my shoes. You've got to be lying. A sin on top of a sin."

"I speak the truth as surely as you."

He was and he wasn't.

What's the truth, the whole truth?
And where's the lie?

THE WHOLE TRUTH

The second student put chickpeas
in his shoes as the rabbi had ordered.
But he didn't tell the other student
that he'd cooked the peas first,
which made them soft and comfortable.

14. A Born Leader

Mulla Nasrudin was constantly having adventures and always loved to brag.

"What can I say?" he told a crowd one day. "I'm a natural-born leader. Why, just last month, as soon as I appeared in front of a tribe of Bedouins, they snapped to attention and followed me."

"In all my years," said an old man, "I've never heard of such leadership!"

Mulla Nasrudin smiled and bowed. "It's a gift."

Every word he said was true, yet what he told was a lie.

What's the truth, the whole truth?
And where's the lie?

THE WHOLE TRUTH

The Bedouins
snapped to attention
and followed him
because he'd just stolen
one of their horses.

15. Pleased to See

A farmer in rural New York was eager to sell his horse.

"Is he healthy?" asked a possible buyer. "Does he pull a good load?"

"Healthy as the best in my family," assured the farmer. "And you'll be pleased to see him pull a load."

Hearing that, the buyer happily paid for the horse. But two days later he was back, demanding that his money be returned.

"That horse of yours is good for nothing. You promised he would pull a good load, but he won't budge with the smallest of wagons. You lied."

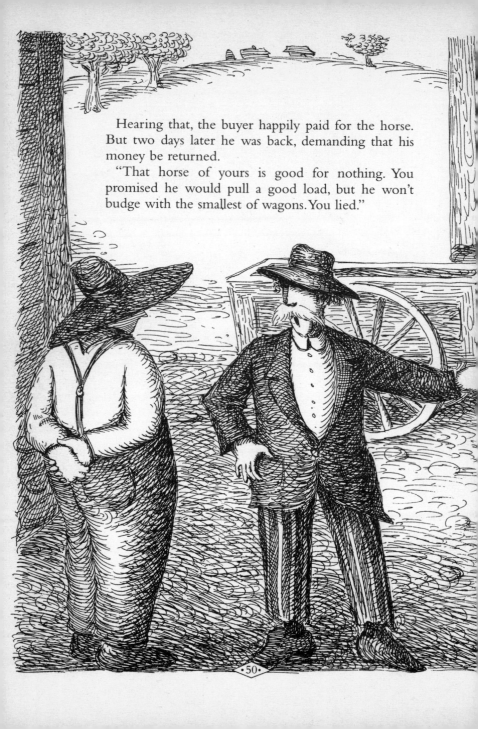

"I spoke the truth," said the farmer, "as always."

"No, you haven't," argued the new owner. "I want my money back."

Both men spoke with honesty, and both were still arguing when the sun began to set.

What's the truth, the whole truth?
And where's the lie?

THE WHOLE TRUTH

The farmer never said the horse
would pull a big load.
He had carefully stated, "You'll be
pleased to see him pull a load."
Knowing that the horse rarely pulled
any load, he knew the new owner
would indeed be pleased if he ever
saw the horse pull a load.

16.
Pockets

A tour guide in the Grand Canyon loved to make bets with the people he took on tours.

One day he told a well-dressed man, "I bet you five dollars I've got more money in my pocket than you have."

"*That* is the most foolish wager you've ever made," said the man as he pulled hundreds of dollars out of his pocket. "I accept."

The tour guide pulled out his five dollars and won the bet because what he'd said was true.

What's the truth, the whole truth?
And where's the lie?

THE WHOLE TRUTH

The tour guide only said,
"I've got more money
in my pocket than you have,"
meaning in his own pocket,
yet he knew the rich man
would leap to the conclusion
that he'd said, "I've got more
money in my pocket than
you have in *your* pocket."
The rich man had no money
in the guide's pocket.

17 · Stolen Yams

Ijapa and his wife, Yanrinbo, were known for
being lazy. They rarely worked in their garden
and never stored food. As a result they often
had nothing to eat.

One day they decided to steal some yams from a neighbor's storehouse. As soon as the neighbor discovered his yams were missing, he suspected Ijapa and his wife. Both were immediately taken before the chief to be questioned and given the traditional herbal drink that tested truth against lies.

"You are charged with stealing yams from your neighbor's storehouse," said the chief.

"My hands have not picked up a single yam," said Ijapa. "I tell the truth. If I'm lying, may I swallow the truth drink and die."

"I, too, tell the truth," said Yanrinbo. "I've never set foot near our neighbor's storehouse. If I'm lying, may I swallow the drink of truth and die."

Both swallowed the traditional drink, but neither died or even fell ill, which proved to all they were telling the truth. Yet the chief was still certain they were both telling lies.

What's the truth, the whole truth?
And where's the lie?

THE WHOLE TRUTH

When the two went
to their neighbor's storehouse,
Ijapa picked no yams.
His wife rode on his shoulders
and took the yams
without *her* feet ever
touching the ground.

18.
Inheritance

An old man who knew he was soon to die asked his two sons to come near his bed.

"The treasure I've struggled to save is buried in the vineyard. It's yours to find and share."

After their father died, the brothers dug in the vineyard from dawn till dusk every day for over a week, but they didn't find a single coin.

"Father lied," the younger brother complained to a friend. "There's not a coin to be found. His final words were only a lie."

That same evening the older brother was celebrating with a friend.

"What a wonderful treasure our father left us in the vineyard. Without his words I wouldn't have found it."

When the younger brother heard of his brother's conversation, he accused him of hoarding the wealth for himself.

What's the truth, the whole truth?
And where's the lie?

THE WHOLE TRUTH

Truth and treasure—like beauty—are often
in the eye of the beholder. It is true the father
left no buried coins, but he never said he did.
"Coins" was the younger brother's definition of
"treasure." The older brother came to understand
that his father's words were true when
the vineyard began to flourish as a result
of all their digging and working the soil.
The vineyard, enriched by their work,
was the treasure.

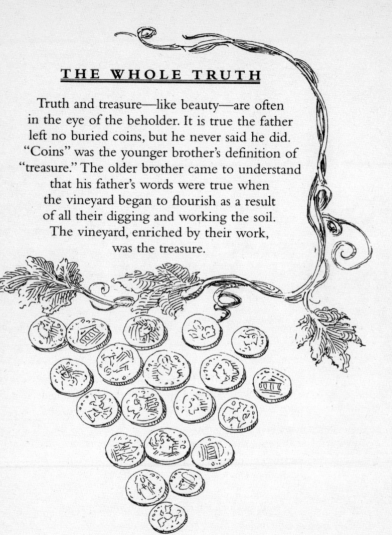

NOTES

1. "One Cookie" is based on Tale Type 1565—The Big Cake, as summarized in *Types and Motifs of the Judeo-Spanish Folktales* by Reginetta Haboucha (New York: Garland, 1992). Flemish and Serbo-Croatian variants are cited in *The Types of the Folktales* by Antti Aarne (translated and enlarged by Stith Thompson, second edition; Helsinki: Folklore Fellows Communications #184, 1961).

2. "The Donkey and the Carrots" is retold from *Master Book of Humorous Illustrations,* compiled and edited by Leewin B. Williams (Nashville: Cokesbury Press, 1938), and "Riddle Me This" in *The Talking Turtle and Other Ozark Folk Tales* edited by Vance Randolph (New York: Columbia University Press, 1957). Randolph collected the tale in 1924 from Pete Woolsey of Missouri, who'd heard it from a farmer in Arkansas.

3. "Ropedancing" is one of many German and Flemish tales about the rascal named Tyll Eulenspiegel. This story is retold from *Tyll Ulenspiegel's Merry Pranks* by M. Jagendorf (New York: Vanguard, 1938) and *The Glorious Adventures of Tyl Ulenspiegl* by Charles de Coster, translated by Allan Ross Macdougall (New York: Pantheon, 1943).

4. "Half the Cherries" is a tale shared among the Pennsylvania Dutch. It is retold from "For the Half" in *Pennsylvania German Folk Tales, Legends, Once-Upon-a-Time Stories, Maxims, and Sayings* by Thomas Brendle and William Troxell (Norristown, Penn.: Pennsylvania German Society, 1944).

5. "A Little Land" is retold from the introduction to *The Folk Literature of the Kurdistani Jews: An Anthology,* edited by Yona Sabar (New Haven: Yale University Press, 1982). Sabar worked from various sources, including *Kĕhillot Yĕhude Kurdistan* by Abraham Ben-Jacob (Jerusalem, 1961). "A Little Land" is a truly international tale; variants have been collected in China, Egypt, Finland, France, Iceland, Northern England, Turkey, and Russia, and from the Wyandot Indians of North America.

6. "A Poor Scholar" is retold from *Jest upon Jest: A Selection from the Jestbooks and Collections of Merry Tales Published from the Reign of Richard III to George III* by John Wardroper (London: Routledge, 1970). Wardroper worked from *Cambridge Jests, or Witty Alarums for Melancholy Spirits. By a Lover of Ha, Ha, He, 1674.*

7. "No Time to Lie" is a popular tale throughout the United States. It is retold from sources including *Who Blowed Up the Church House? and Other Ozark Tales,* edited by Vance Randolph (New York: Columbia University Press, 1952) and "Pennsylvania Fairylore and Folktales" by Herbert Halpert in *Journal of American Folklore,* Volume 58 (1945). Variants have also been collected in Ireland, India, Germany, Estonia, China, and Finland.

8. "Lost Money" is retold from the Puerto Rican tale summarized under Tale Type 1556A—Rascal Finds Bag of Money in *The Types of the Folktale in Cuba, Puerto Rico, the Dominican Republic, and Spanish South America* by Terrence Leslie Hansen (Berkeley, Calif.: University of California Press, 1957). Hansen worked from *Raíces de la tierra: Colección de cuentos populares y tradiciones* by María Cadilla de Martínez (Arecibo, 1941).

9. "All Mine" is retold from *Mules and Men* by Zora Neale Hurston (Philadelphia: Lippincott, 1935) and *Storytellers: Folktales and Legends from the South*, edited by John A. Burrison (Athens, Ga.: University of Georgia Press, 1989, 1991). Burrison's variant was collected from Emily Ellis of northwest Georgia.

10. "Matti and Peikko" is retold from *Tales from a Finnish Tupa* by James Cloyd Bowman and Margery Bianco (from a translation from the Finnish by Aili Kolehmainen; Chicago: Whitman, 1940) and *Folk-tales of Kashmir* by J. Hinton Knowles (London, 1893). Variants have also been collected in Cuba, Denmark, Turkey, Italy, Holland, Ethiopia, Argentina, England, and the former Czechoslovakia.

11. "A Tall Hog" is an English tale retold from *Shakespeare Jest-Books*, Volume Three, edited by William C. Hazlitt (London, 1864).

12. "Love and Pumpkins" is retold from *Filipino Popular Tales* by Dean S. Fansler (Memoirs of the American Folklore Society, XII; New York: American Folk-lore Society, 1921) and *Village Folk-Tales of Ceylon*, Volume Two, collected and translated by H. Parker (Dehiwala, Ceylon: Tisara Press, 1910).

13. "Shoes and Peas" is retold from "Merry Mismash from Old Europe," in *Encyclopedia of Jewish Humor: From Biblical Times to the Modern Age*, compiled by Henry D. Spalding (New York: Jonathan David Publishers, 1969). Spalding gives no sources.

14. "A Born Leader" is retold from *The Exploits of the Incomparable Mulla Nasrudin* by Indries Shah (New York: Simon and Schuster, 1966). Shah gives no sources. There are countless tales in the Middle East about the foolishness and clever tricks of the man known as Mulla Nasrudin or the Hodja.

15. "Pleased to See" is a tale shared in New York State. It is retold from *Body, Boots and Britches* by Harold W. Thompson (Philadelphia: Lippincott, 1940) and *Listen for a Lonesome Drum: A York State Chronicle* by Carl Carmer (New York: Farrar, 1936).

16. "Pockets" is retold from Chapter One in *Highways and Byways of the Pacific Coast*, a traveler's study of land and lore by Clifton Johnson (New York: Macmillan, 1908).

17. "Stolen Yams" is retold from *Olode the Hunter and Other Tales from Nigeria* by Harold Courlander with Ezekiel A. Eshugbayi (New York: Harcourt, 1968). Ijapa is traditionally portrayed as a tortoise in Yoruba tales. The Manipur variant in *Folktales of India*, edited by Brenda E. F. Beck (Chicago: University of Chicago Press, 1987), features two young men.

18. "Inheritance" is retold from one of Aesop's fables, often titled "The Farmer and His Sons," and Number 9, Specimen II in *Linguistic Survey of India*, Volume Seven, compiled and edited by G. A. Grierson (Delhi: Motilal Banarsidass, 1905). Variants also exist in Spain, Lithuania, and Slovenia.